Puppy Friends™ #7

Nipper the Noisy Puppy

by Jenny Dale

Illustrated by Frank Rodgers

Aladdin Paperbacks
New York   London   Toronto   Sydney   Singapore

Look for these PUPPY FRIENDS books!

#1 *Gus the Greedy Puppy*
#2 *Lily the Lost Puppy*
#3 *Spot the Sporty Puppy*
#4 *Lenny the Lazy Puppy*
#5 *Max the Muddy Puppy*
#6 *Billy the Brave Puppy*

Coming soon

#8 *Tilly the Tidy Puppy*
#9 *Spike the Special Puppy*

Special thanks to Narinder Dhami

First Aladdin Paperbacks edition February 2001

Text copyright © 1999 by Working Partners Limited
Illustrations copyright © 1999 by Frank Rodgers
First published 1999 by Macmillan Children's Books U.K.
Created by Working Partners Limited

Aladdin Paperbacks
An imprint of Simon & Schuster Children's Publishing Division
1230 Avenue of the Americas
New York, NY 10020

Library of Congress Catalog Card Number: 20-010862
ISBN 0-689-83974-X

Chapter One

"Four-nothing! Four-nothing!" Adam chanted as he acted out scoring the winning goal again.

Adam's mom, Mrs. Roberts, was waiting in front of the school. "Hi, Mom!" Adam called. "We played Mr. King's class at soccer this afternoon. They didn't stand a chance!"

"Adam scored two of the goals, Mrs. Roberts," said Daniel.

"He was excellent!" Ben added.

Daniel Carter and Ben Lewis were Adam's best friends. The three boys were always at one another's houses, playing soccer. Ben and Daniel were going to Adam's for the afternoon.

Mrs. Roberts smiled. "It sounds like you're quite a hero today, Adam."

Adam turned pink. He loved soccer and wanted to play for his favorite team when he grew up.

"I wish I was good at soccer," Ben grumbled as they all crossed the road. "I've never scored a goal in my life!"

"It might help if you didn't keep falling

over your feet," Daniel pointed out.

Ben grinned and nodded. "Maybe I'd be better in goal . . ."

But Adam wasn't listening to what Ben was saying. He'd suddenly noticed a man walking down the street toward them with a big Alsatian dog on a leash. Adam's heart began to pound, and his knees felt like they'd turned to water.

Adam didn't like dogs. When he was four years old, a big, cranky old dog had snapped at him when he'd gone to pat it. Adam had been terrified. He'd never forgotten it and had been scared of dogs ever since.

Ben and Daniel were still telling Mrs. Roberts about the game, but Adam didn't join in. As the man and the dog came nearer, he slipped quickly behind his mom, out of the way. The Alsatian had big sharp teeth and a long pink tongue, and it looked a little like the picture of the wolf in the story of Red Riding Hood that Adam's mom had read to him years ago.

The man and the dog went by, and Adam heaved a silent sigh of relief. Not even his mom knew just how much dogs scared him, although she'd noticed that he didn't like them. Adam didn't want *anyone* to know—especially Daniel and Ben. They'd think he was a real wimp.

"Oh, Adam, I forgot to tell you," said his mom. "The new neighbors are moving in next door today."

As they turned onto their street, Adam saw a large truck parked near their house. Men in overalls were hurrying in and out of the house next door, carrying chairs, tables, lamps, and bookcases.

"Have you seen the new people?" Adam asked eagerly. "What are they like?" Their old neighbor, Mrs. Miller, had been very nice, but Adam was hoping that someone he could play with might come and live next door.

"I've only said a quick hello," his mom replied. "Their last name is Taylor. They've got a baby and—"

"What an awful noise!" Ben interrupted, putting his hands over his ears as they got closer to the house and heard frantic barking.

"That dog is deafening! It sounds really fierce," Daniel added, doing the same.

"Ah, that's what I was going to say." Mrs. Roberts smiled. "They also have a very noisy dog!"

"A . . . dog?" Adam repeated, in what he hoped was a normal-sounding voice.

"Nipper!" The front door of the next-door house stood open. Inside, a man was shouting at the top of his voice. "Nipper! Will you *please* be quiet!"

Ben and Daniel began to laugh.

"Nipper?" said Ben. "That's a funny name!"

"He must *nip* people," Daniel pointed out, and they both laughed even harder. "You'll have to watch out, Adam!"

Adam tried to smile, but he was almost frozen to the spot with fear. *A dog next door?* And from the sound of the barking, it was a big, fierce-looking dog with long, pointed teeth and a terrible growl. . . .

Adam's heart thumped as his mom unlocked their front door. Every second he was expecting to see a huge, angry dog charge out of the Taylors' open front door and rush toward them, growling. Having a scary dog was his worst nightmare. But this wasn't a dream. It was horribly real.

Chapter Two

The dog was even bigger and fiercer than Adam had imagined. It was jet-black and it had huge, fiery eyes and sharp white teeth.

"Go away!" Adam croaked in a scared voice. "Leave me alone!"

The dog didn't take any notice. It began to growl deep in its throat, drawing its lips back in a snarl. Then it ran straight toward Adam. . . .

Adam gasped and sat bolt upright in bed. The sun was streaming through the curtains. He blinked a few times, then sank back against his pillow. He'd been having a bad dream, a nightmare about

Nipper, the dog who'd moved in next door.

Nipper was barking again now, and although Adam could only hear him faintly, it was still enough to make him shudder.

"Adam!" his mom called up the stairs. "Time to get up or you'll be late for school."

Adam leaped out of bed. He wasn't that crazy about school usually, but at least there wouldn't be any frightening dogs there. He washed and dressed quickly, then went downstairs.

"Isn't that dog ever going to stop barking? It's really driving me crazy!" grumbled Adam's dad, who liked peace and quiet at breakfast time.

"Oh, he'll be all right when he settles in," Adam's mom replied. "He's probably just barking at the milkman."

There was silence for a few minutes, then the barking started again.

"I bet he's barking at the mailman now!" snorted Mr. Roberts.

"Or the paperboy," said Adam's mom. "Mr. Taylor told me that Nipper's already a very good guard dog."

"Have you seen Nipper, Mom?" Adam asked in a small voice.

"No, not yet." Mrs. Roberts glanced at him as if she'd guessed why he was asking. "But Mrs. Taylor told me he's still just a puppy."

Adam wasn't convinced. Nipper didn't *sound* like a puppy. Then he began to feel even more alarmed. If Nipper was already scary as a puppy, what would he be like when he was fully grown?

"Time to go, Adam." Mrs. Roberts went to get her coat. "Don't forget your bag. You've got karate after school, don't you?"

Adam nodded. That meant he'd be home late—which was great, because then there would be less chance of meeting Nipper.

"I'm sure Nipper's very friendly, Adam," his mom said gently as they went outside. "After all, the Taylors have a baby. They wouldn't be able to keep Nipper if he was a dangerous dog."

Adam didn't say anything. Nipper might be friendly to the Taylors and their baby—but that didn't mean he was going to be friendly toward Adam!

In the Taylors' hall, Nipper was patrolling up and down behind the front door. He'd already had to scare off three intruders this morning. Two of them had actually pushed things through the mail slot!

Suddenly Nipper stiffened. What's that? he thought. He could hear sounds and strange voices nearby, and he could smell strange smells!

"Alert! Alert! Strangers approaching!" he barked to the Taylors.

"Rouurrouff . . . rrouu rrouu . . . rouu-roufff!"

Adam nearly leaped out of his skin. He and his mom were just coming out of their house. If his mom hadn't been with him, he would have dived back inside and shut the door. Instead, he ran down the path, looking anxiously over his shoulder to make sure Nipper hadn't escaped.

"It's all right, Adam," his mom said calmly. "I'm sure Nipper's bark is worse than his bite."

"So has he bitten lots of people?"

Adam asked nervously. It was just what he'd been scared of.

"No, silly, it means that just because Nipper barks a lot, he isn't necessarily going to bite you!" his mom explained.

"Maybe we should go over and meet him sometime. . . ."

Adam didn't say anything. There was *no way* he was going to go into the Taylors' house and get attacked by an angry dog! As far as he was concerned, it would be just fine if he never set eyes on nasty Nipper. . . .

The next day was Saturday. Daniel and Ben came over to do some soccer practice. They all went out into the backyard as usual, but Adam couldn't help feeling nervous. He'd heard Nipper barking loudly again last night *and* this morning. What if the Taylors let Nipper out into *their* backyard at the same time? Was there any way the dog could get at him?

Adam looked at the fence between the two yards. It was really high. Nipper would have to be as big as a horse to jump over that! But what if the bushes in front of the fence were hiding a hole that Nipper could squeeze through? What if he tunneled underneath? Adam checked the fence behind all the bushes. It seemed sturdy enough.

"Hey, Adam!" Ben called impatiently. "You're half asleep! Are we going to play soccer or not?"

"Sorry." Adam ran to get his soccer ball from the garage.

"Adam, I'm just popping next door to see Mrs. Taylor," Mrs. Roberts called out the back door. "She wants to borrow a screwdriver."

"All right," Adam said. As long as she didn't want *him* to go next door!

Just then the telephone began to ring in the hall. "Oh, that's sure to be your grandma, Adam," Mrs. Roberts said with a sigh. "And I really don't have time to stop and chat, either."

"We'll go next door for you, Mrs. Roberts," Daniel offered politely.

Adam froze in shock.

"Well, thank you, Daniel," Mrs. Roberts said, glancing at Adam. "But I don't want to spoil your game. . . ."

"No problem," said Ben. "We don't mind, do we, Adam?"

Adam looked at Daniel and Ben. What could he do? If he said no, they'd want to know why. . . . "No," he muttered, "we don't mind at all."

Chapter Three

"Come on, then," Daniel said, heading for the gate that led through the fence between the two houses.

"Do you think we might get to meet Noisy Nipper?" Ben said, laughing, as he followed.

"Just a minute," Adam said. His throat was so dry, he could hardly get the words out. "Why don't you two stay here—figure out what we're going to use for goals?"

Adam couldn't go next door with Daniel and Ben. He just couldn't. What if he came face-to-face with Nipper and made a fool of himself in front of them? He'd never live it down. . . .

Daniel shrugged. "Good idea—it'll save you some time."

"Okay, see you in a minute, then," Ben said, kicking the ball to Daniel.

Adam walked slowly toward the fence. He could hardly believe what he was about to do. But *anything* was better than looking stupid in front of his friends.

He paused by the gate. Maybe he could just push the screwdriver through the mail slot. Or leave it outside on the step. Nipper might even be out for a walk with Mr. or Mrs. Taylor, and then there wouldn't be a problem. . . .

Nipper yawned and sprawled out more comfortably on the rug at the bottom of the stairs. It had quickly become his favorite place to sleep in the new house. It was the best place to keep an eye out for any intruders. If anyone came to the Taylors' front door, Nipper would know about it and immediately be on guard to scare them away!

Suddenly Nipper pricked up his ears and growled softly. WAS THAT THE SOUND OF HIS FRONT GATE OPENING?

Adam walked around to the front of the house and up the path to the Taylors' front door, telling himself there was nothing to be scared of. It didn't work, though, because he was shaking like jelly.

Halfway up the path, Adam stopped. He thought he could hear a sort of clicking noise from inside the house. His heart racing, Adam listened hard. No, he must have imagined it. . . .

Nipper trotted across the hall, his claws clicking on the polished wooden floorboards. He stopped by the front door and sniffed suspiciously. He could definitely smell a stranger on the other side. And the scent was getting stronger. . . .

Adam forced himself to keep going until he finally made it to the Taylors' front door. There was still no sign of Nipper. Adam let out a huge sigh of relief. The dog must have been taken out for a walk, he decided, and feeling much more cheerful, he reached out to ring the doorbell. . . .

Chapter Four

"ROURR ROURR . . . ROURR ROURR . . . ROURR ROUFFF!"

Adam sprang back, tripped over his feet, and fell onto his backside. He got up again right away, glancing around to see if anyone had noticed. But the street was empty. He looked back at the front door, half expecting Nipper to knock it down flat and come charging toward him.

In the Taylors' hallway, Nipper scrabbled furiously at the door. "I know you're out there!" he barked. "Who are you? And what do you want with my family?"

Trembling, Adam looked around for the screwdriver, which had gone flying when he'd tripped. It was in a nearby flower bed, squashing a clump of marigolds.

He picked up the screwdriver and began to back away. He'd tell his mom that Mr. and Mrs. Taylor weren't in. It might be a fib, but that was better than coming face-to-face with an angry dog. . . .

"Be quiet, Nipper!" Adam jumped as he heard Mrs. Taylor's voice from behind the front door. So there *was* someone home.

"Hello?" Mrs. Taylor called. "Could you wait just a minute, please?"

Adam stood uncertainly, wondering what to do. He still had a chance to get away before Mrs. Taylor opened the door and the dreaded Nipper charged out, baring his teeth!

Then another sound behind him made him jump again. His soccer ball had suddenly come flying over the fence and was bouncing into the Taylors' front yard. The next second the gate opened, and Daniel and Ben ran through, chasing after the ball.

"Ben was trying to show off his skill!" Daniel said, running into the Taylors' front yard. "What's up, Adam? Aren't they in?"

"No," Adam muttered.

"Nipper's in, though, by the sound of it!" Ben added with a grin.

Then, just as Adam reached the gate, the Taylors' front door opened.

"Oh, hello," Mrs. Taylor called with a smile. "You must be Adam. Come in."

"Hello," Adam said weakly. Now he was really trapped.

Daniel and Ben collected the soccer ball and went off to continue their game.

Adam braced himself, waiting for a large, black, snarling animal to streak past Mrs. Taylor and head straight for him. But nothing happened. Although Adam could still hear frantic barking, there was no sign of Nipper.

"Sorry I kept you waiting," Mrs. Taylor went on, "but I had to shut Nipper in the kitchen. He's such a nuisance if he gets out."

Adam imagined Mrs. Taylor dragging a large, growling dog down the hallway and into the kitchen. But he cheered up a little when he heard that Nipper had been shut away.

"LET ME OUT!" Nipper howled from behind the kitchen door. "I've got important things to do!" It was his duty to protect his family from danger. No one was allowed inside the house unless he'd personally checked them out first!

Then Nipper sniffed the air suspiciously.

The person who'd been standing OUTSIDE his house was now INSIDE! Nipper didn't like that AT ALL.

"Rouurrouff . . . rrouu rrouu . . . ROUR-ROURROUFFF!"

"Oh, be quiet, Nipper!" called Mrs. Taylor. "It's so nice to meet you at last, Adam," she said, welcoming him in. She glanced at the screwdriver in his hand. "Is that for me? How wonderful—we seem to have lost the toolbox, and so many things need fixing!"

"Yes." Adam handed over the screwdriver, peering uneasily down the hallway at the kitchen door. "My mom says you can keep it as long as you like—"

He was interrupted by a loud wail from upstairs.

"Oh, dear, I thought the baby was fast asleep." Mrs. Taylor sighed. "I bet Nipper's barking woke him up! I won't be a minute, Adam."

She hurried up the stairs. Adam waited anxiously, his eyes still fixed on

the kitchen door. Nipper had stopped barking now, but Adam could hear the dog sniffing and snuffling and scratching, which was just as scary!

"I've got to get out of here!" Nipper whined, doing his very best to pull the door open. "My family needs me!"

Adam blinked. For a moment he'd thought . . . no, his eyes must be playing tricks on him. He thought he'd seen the kitchen door move. . . .

Adam told himself that not even a big, strong dog could open a door that had been closed. But as he stared hard at the door, it moved again! Adam's heart began to beat so fast, it banged against his ribs like a drum. Somehow the dog was managing to pull the kitchen door open. It hadn't been shut properly. Nipper would soon be free!

Chapter Five

The kitchen door was nudged open a couple of inches now.

Adam panicked. He ran over to the front door and tried to pull it open, but the lock was stuck and Adam's hands were shaking so much, he couldn't turn it. But he *had* to get away!

In desperation, Adam rushed up the

stairs and onto the Taylors' landing!

"Adam?" Mrs. Taylor came out of the baby's room, looking surprised. "What's the matter?"

Adam's teeth were chattering so much, he could hardly speak. "Your dog opened the kitchen door!" he gasped.

"Oh, I must not have closed it all the way," Mrs. Taylor said, shaking her

head. "It has to be slammed shut really hard or it comes open again. There are so many things that need repairing in this house. It'll take us ages to fix them all—" Then she broke off and looked more closely at Adam. "Are you all right?"

"F-F-Fine," Adam answered, trying to sound cool and calm.

"You're not scared of Nipper, are you?" Mrs. Taylor raised her eyebrows. "I know he makes a terrible noise, but he's really very friendly."

Adam didn't look at all convinced.

"I'll tell you what, I'll go down and let Nipper into the backyard," Mrs. Taylor said kindly.

"I'm not scared of Nipper, really,"

Adam muttered, feeling very ashamed. He didn't like anyone knowing just how frightened he was of dogs.

"Well, I'll put Nipper out, anyway," Mrs. Taylor replied as she went downstairs. "Then at least the baby can get some sleep!"

Nipper finally managed to get the kitchen door open. Panting hard, he dashed out into the hallway, sniffing every inch of it as he went. He knew that a stranger had passed that way, and he was determined to find out exactly who it was!

"Very interesting!" Nipper growled softly to himself as he sniffed his way over to the front door. "Whoever that person is, he's still

here—and I think he's upstairs!"

Nipper headed for the stairs . . .

. . . only to be stopped in his tracks by Mrs. Taylor coming down them.

"You bad boy, Nipper!" she scolded him, taking hold of his collar firmly. "Now, come on. I'm going to put you in the backyard for a while."

"But I don't want to go into the yard!" Nipper barked sulkily. "I want to protect you from the intruder!"

"Now, don't be silly, Nipper," Mrs. Taylor said firmly. "You know you love going outside. You're just being a nuisance." She put him out and closed the back door.

"Let me in!" Nipper barked furiously.

"Thank you again for bringing the screwdriver around, Adam," Mrs. Taylor said as Adam came cautiously down the stairs. "Say thank you to your mom for me, won't you?"

Adam nodded. "Nice to meet you," he said, hurrying over to the front door. He'd spent enough time with Nipper for one day!

"Oh, no!" Mrs. Taylor groaned as the baby started crying again upstairs. "Can you let yourself out, Adam? Give the front door a good pull because it's a bit stuck."

"I know!" Adam said to himself as Mrs. Taylor went upstairs again. He took hold of the lock and pulled hard, but it took him a moment or two to wrestle the door open.

Nipper was tired of waiting to be let back into the house. He trotted around the yard, wondering whether he should dig up the juicy bone he'd buried in the flower bed the day he'd arrived in this new place.

"But if I do dig it up," Nipper growled suspiciously, "that person who's in my house might try to steal it!"

Nipper decided to leave the bone where it was. He could hear noises coming from the

yard next door, and he could smell more strange people running around, although he couldn't see them because the fence was too high. They might want to steal his bone, too!

Then Nipper pricked up his ears. He'd heard the sound of his family's front door closing! Nipper's tail began to quiver, and he dashed over to the fence at the side of the house. . . .

Closing the Taylor's front door behind him, Adam breathed a sigh of relief. But his knees were still shaking so much, he wasn't sure he'd be able to play soccer now. He just hoped that Mrs. Taylor wouldn't say anything to his mom about what had happened—

CRACK!

Nipper hurled himself at the fence. Part of the wood was rotting near the bottom and it cracked, leaving a hole. . . .

"What was *that?*" Adam said. For a second he thought Ben or Daniel must

have kicked the soccer ball into the greenhouse and cracked a pane of glass. But the next moment something came racing around the side of the Taylors' house and straight toward him!

Chapter Six

It was a dog! But it wasn't the fierce dog of Adam's nightmare. Adam stood rooted to the spot, staring at a plump little puppy.

This was Noisy Nipper?

"Hello there!" Nipper barked. "I need to find out if you're a friend or not!"

Adam swallowed hard. Was Nipper

going to bite him? Adam wanted to call for help, but he couldn't get a single word out.

Holding his breath, Adam watched as the puppy circled around him, sniffing his soccer cleats and ankles. With a patch of black fur over one eye, Nipper looked like a doggy pirate. The rest of his chunky little body was a soft, snowy white.

After a while, Nipper's short, stumpy tail began to wag a little. Adam remembered something his mom had once said. "If a dog wags its tail, it wants to make friends with you." Adam breathed out.

Nipper's tail began to wag harder. "Yes, you seem to be all right," he

barked. "In fact, I think we should be friends!" And he jumped up, putting his two front paws on Adam's knees.

Adam was so shocked, he almost fell over backwards.

"Aren't you going to say hello to me?" Nipper barked. He stared up at Adam hopefully.

Adam still felt scared. But even though he didn't know much about dogs, he could see that Nipper was trying to be friendly.

"Hello, Nipper," he said in a shaky voice. Then he cautiously patted the top of the puppy's head.

Nipper immediately went mad with joy, barking and pawing at Adam's knees.

Adam felt very nervous but proud of himself, though he couldn't help jumping when Nipper licked his hand!

"Nipper?" The Taylors' gate suddenly opened, and Mrs. Taylor appeared.

"Adam! Are you all right?" she asked, concerned, when she saw Nipper leaping around him.

Adam nodded, still stroking the puppy. "I'm fine!" he said. And it was true. Looking down at the bundle of energy that was trying to lick his knees to death, Adam had to admit that Nipper wasn't nearly as scary as he had imagined.

"That fence is falling to pieces!" Mrs. Taylor sighed. "No wonder Nipper managed to smash his way through it! Still," she said, smiling, "you two seem to have made friends now!"

"We certainly have!" Nipper barked happily. "I've checked him over, and I think he's great!"

Adam still couldn't quite believe what had happened. He'd been scared of dogs for so long—and now here he was, making friends with one!

"What kind of dog is Nipper?" Adam asked as he bent down to pat the puppy again.

"A bull terrier," Mrs. Taylor replied. "He's a real softie, despite the terrible noise he makes. Maybe you'd like to take him for a walk sometime, Adam? Oh, and he likes playing soccer, too."

"So do I!" Adam said. He thought for a few seconds, then made up his mind. "Er . . . do you think Nipper would like to come next door now and play soccer with me and my friends?"

"I'm sure he would!" Mrs. Taylor bent down and ruffled Nipper's ears. "Wouldn't you, boy?" she said.

Nipper licked her chin and barked in agreement.

A few minutes later Adam walked into his backyard with Nipper trotting beside him on his leash.

Adam was a little nervous because he'd never walked a dog before and Nipper wasn't exactly very well trained. The puppy kept grabbing the leash in his mouth and shaking it from side to side, trying to pull it out of Adam's hand. He thought that was a great game.

Adam couldn't help laughing. He'd

never realized before that dogs could be fun!

"Hey, who's this?" Daniel asked as he and Ben ran across the yard to meet them. "Is this Noisy Nipper?"

Ben kneeled down and stroked the plump little puppy, who was clearly loving all the attention. "Hello, Nipper!"

"He's come to play soccer with us," Adam told them.

"Adam!" Mrs. Roberts rushed out of the kitchen, her eyes wide. "That's a dog!"

"Yes, Mom, it's Nipper!" Adam said proudly. "I made friends with him when I went next door, and Mrs. Taylor said I can take Nipper for walks and play with him whenever I want to."

Mrs. Roberts looked as if she could hardly believe her ears. "Well, that's great, Adam," she said. "It looks like Nipper's very fond of you already!"

Even though Ben and Daniel were still fussing over the puppy, Nipper was pawing at Adam's leg, wanting Adam to stroke him. It made Adam feel really special.

"Come on, Nipper!" Adam ran for the ball and kicked it across the yard. "It's you and me against Dan and Ben!"

Nipper raced after Adam. "You're on!" he barked happily.

"I don't think I'll be so scared of dogs

from now on. Some of them might be as nice as you!" Adam whispered as they ran across the yard together. "And Mom was right—your bark *is* worse than your bite!"

If you like horses, friends, fun, and excitement, then you'll love

Sheltie

The little pony with the big heart!

written and illustrated by Peter Clover

JOIN SHELTIE AND EMMA IN THEIR MANY THRILLING ADVENTURES TOGETHER!

#1 Sheltie the Shetland Pony
0-689-83574-4/$3.99

#2 Sheltie Saves the Day!
0-689-83575-2/$3.99

#3 Sheltie and the Runaway
0-689-83576-0/$3.99

#4 Sheltie Finds a Friend
0-689-83975-8/$3.99

#5 Sheltie to the Rescue
0-689-83976-6/$3.99

#6 Sheltie in Danger
0-689-84028-4/$3.99

Everyone needs Kitten Friends!

Fluffy and fun, purry and huggable, what could be more perfect than a kitten?

by
Jenny Dale

#1 Felix the Fluffy Kitten
0-689-84108-6 $3.99

#2 Bob the Bouncy Kitten
0-689-84109-4 $3.99

#3 Star the Snowy Kitten
0-689-84110-8 $3.99

#4 Nell the Naughty Kitten
0-689-84029-2 $3.99

#5 Leo the Lucky Kitten
0-689-84030-6 $3.99

#6 Patch the Perfect Kitten
0-689-84031-4 $3.99

ALADDIN PAPERBACKS
Simon & Schuster Children's Publishing
www.SimonSaysKids.com

Everyone needs Puppy Friends!

Bouncy and cute, furry and huggable, what could be more perfect than a puppy?

by
Jenny Dale

#1 Gus the Greedy Puppy
0-689-83423-3 $3.99

#2 Lily the Lost Puppy
0-689-83404-7 $3.99

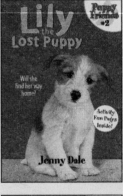

#3 Spot the Sporty Puppy
0-689-83424-1 $3.99

#4 Lenny the Lazy Puppy
0-689-83552-3 $3.99

#5 Max the Muddy Puppy
0-689-83553-1 $3.99

#6 Billy the Brave Puppy
0-689-83554-X $3.99

#7 Nipper the Noisy Puppy
0-689-83974-X $3.99

ALADDIN PAPERBACKS
Simon & Schuster Children's Publishing
www.SimonSaysKids.com